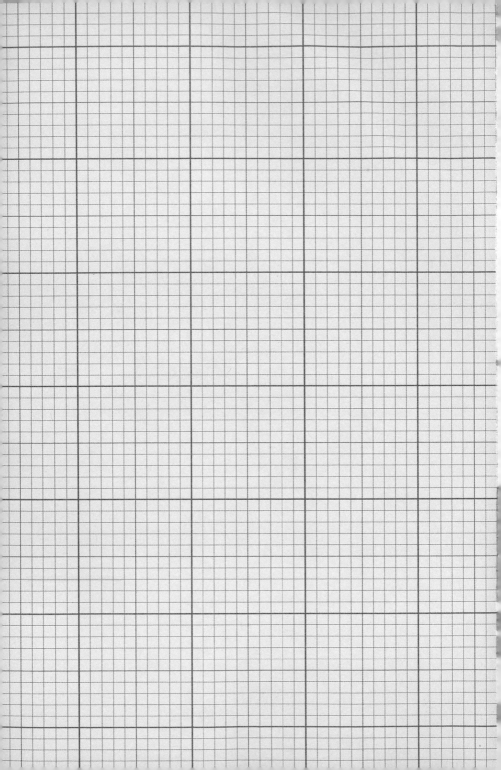

THIS NOTEBOOK BELONGS TO:

Ada

THE QUESTIONEERS SERIES

ADA
TWIST

AND THE DISAPPEARING DOGS

From the **#1** *New York Times* **bestselling creators**
Andrea Beaty **and** David Roberts
with interior illustrations by Jennifer Naalchigar

AMULET BOOKS
NEW YORK

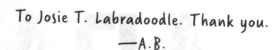

To Josie T. Labradoodle. Thank you.
—A.B.

PUBLISHER'S NOTE: This is a work of fiction. Names, characters, places, and incidents are either the product of the author's imagination or used fictitiously, and any resemblance to actual persons, living or dead, business establishments, events, or locales is entirely coincidental.

Cataloging-in-Publication Data has been applied for and may be obtained from the Library of Congress.

ISBN 978-1-4197-4352-8

Text © 2022 Andrea Beaty
Illustrations © 2022 David Roberts
Interior illustrations by Jennifer Naalchigar
Book design by Heather Kelly

Printed and bound in USA
10 9 8 7 6 5 4 3 2 1

Amulet Books are available at special discounts when purchased in quantity for premiums and promotions as well as fundraising or educational use. Special editions can also be created to specification. For details, contact specialsales@abramsbooks.com or the address below.

Amulet Books® is a registered trademark of Harry N. Abrams, Inc.

ABRAMS The Art of Books
195 Broadway, New York, NY 10007
abramsbooks.com

CHAPTER I

A da Twist pressed her face against the glass display case.

"Zowie!" she said, admiring an enormous tooth resting on a red velvet cloth. The tooth was very old. Very long. And very, VERY sharp. It was a dinosaur tooth. An *Allosaurus* tooth to be exact.

Ada exhaled and a cloud of fog spread over the glass.

"That Allosaurus tooth is 150 million years old!" said Aunt Bernice. "Can you imagine?"

"Zowie," Ada repeated. "Did dinosaurs have dentists? How did the dinosaur get buried? How big was the shovel that dug it out? Did it have feathers? The dinosaur, I mean. Not the shovel."

Aunt Bernice laughed. "Ada," she said, "you always make me think!"

Ada loved helping her great-aunt Bernice at the Can You Dig It? shop, though she spent more time fogging the cases than cleaning them. The shop had every kind of treasure that could be

dug from the Earth. There was always something amazing to discover.

"I almost forgot," said Aunt Bernice. "Your mom needs cat food from the pet shop next door. Let's get it and grab an ice cream while we're out."

"You've got a sweet tooth *and* a dinosaur tooth!" said Ada.

Aunt Bernice laughed again and grabbed her keys. Ada flipped the **BE RIGHT BACK** sign on the door then stepped outside onto the stoop. The sunshine was blinding after the dim light of the shop. Ada squeezed her eyes shut, took a step, and—

"Watch out!"

Ada opened her eyes . . .

BAM!

It was too late. A girl in a blue dress slammed into her, sending them both tumbling into a heap on the sidewalk.

CHAPTER 2

Eeeek!"

A girl in a red polka-dot headscarf ran toward them. It was Rosie Revere. She came to a screeching halt as Ada and Sofia Valdez sat up and brushed themselves off.

"Phew," said Rosie, trying to catch her breath. "Are you okay?"

Ada and Sofia nodded as Rosie helped them to their feet.

"I wasn't looking where I was going!" said Ada. "I'm sorry, Sofia!"

"I'm sorry, too," said Sofia. "I was running too fast to stop."

"Where are you going?" asked Ada.

"We're looking for Pup!" said Sofia. "He's gone!" She blinked back a tear.

"Oh no!" said Ada. "Maybe he chased a squirrel to the park. You know how he loves squirrels!"

Sofia gave a hopeful smile, hugged Ada, and ran down the block with Rosie on her heels. They passed the Pet Palace, narrowly missing a clerk in a deep purple coat, who was loading large bags into a wagon.

"Hello, Bernice!" called a thin woman in a black-and-white flowered coat. She was holding the handle of the wagon.

"Beverly Elaine!" said Aunt Bernice. "How are you?" Aunt Bernice introduced her to Ada. "Ms.

Beverly Elaine Good is one of the best choral teachers ever," she said.

Ms. Good blushed. "You are too kind, Bernice," she said, "but I'm not teaching anymore. I retired."

"Congratulations!" said Aunt Bernice. "You must be busy with all kinds of fun."

Before Ms. Good could answer, a blue-eyed Siberian husky sneaked up behind her and bit down on the corner of her purse. Ms. Good gently tugged the purse away and shook her head.

"He's always trying to get the treats in my purse," she said. She looked sternly at the dog, who looked away innocently. "Oh, Nicky! You're a handful."

"He's beautiful," said the clerk, pulling a triangular pet treat from her pocket. She held the treat out to Nicky, who gobbled it down.

"Say, 'thank you,' Nicky," said Ms. Good.

Nicky made a grumbly, rumbly sound.

"Nicky!" Ms. Good scolded. "Give me a note."

Ms. Good tilted her head upward and sang the most perfect note: "*LAAAAAAAAAAAAAAAAA.*"

Nicky tilted his head and howled. *WOOOOOOOOOOOOOOOOF!*

Ada laughed.

"He's not the best singer in the bunch," said Ms. Good with a wink, "but he tries." She scratched Nicky's chin. "The pet shop loads up my wagon, so I don't have to go inside," she said.

She leaned closer to Ada and whispered, "I don't like the fish."

"The fish?" asked Ada.

Ms. Good made a face. "The fish tanks are so . . . well . . . fishy!"

The clerk loaded the last bag onto the wagon, handed Ms. Good a receipt, and sneaked another treat to Nicky.

"Lovely meeting you, Ada," said Ms. Good. "Bernice, shall we grab a coffee tomorrow?"

"I'd love that!" said Aunt Bernice.

Ms. Good headed down the sidewalk, singing as she went. Nicky trotted happily behind the wagon, singing right along.

Wooof! Wooooof! Wooooooooooooof!

A moment later, they turned the corner and were gone.

CHAPTER 3

Ada and Aunt Bernice went inside the Pet Palace. While Aunt Bernice looked at cat food, Ada looked at the fish tanks. They were fishy, but Ada still liked them. She was looking at a very fat goldfish when Iggy Peck came in with a piece of paper.

"Hi, Iggy!" said Ada.

"Hey," Iggy said sadly.

"What's wrong?" asked Ada.

"Bricks is missing!" said Iggy. "I made a sign

to hang on the bulletin board in case somebody sees him."

Iggy showed Ada the paper. It was a drawing of his cat, Bricks, inside a very fancy house. Large letters read: **LOST CAT!**

"I drew Bricks in this house because he loves Victorian architecture as much as I do," said Iggy.

Ada wasn't listening. She was looking at something behind Iggy.

"That's weird," said Ada. "That's really, really weird."

"Is it?" asked Iggy. "Do you think he'd like Gothic architecture better?"

"No, Iggy," said Ada. "Look!"

She pointed to the wall behind Iggy. Slowly, he turned around. His eyes opened wide.

"Wha—?" he said.

Every inch of the wall was plastered with pictures of lost dogs. Some had been missing for months. Others just a few days.

"The dogs are disappearing!" said Ada.

Iggy looked at his poster. "Not just dogs," he said.

"I think Blue River Creek has a problem," said Ada.

"I think Blue River Creek has something worse than a problem," said Iggy. "It has a pet thief!"

CHAPTER 4

"O ver here!" called a familiar voice as Ada and Iggy stepped into Herbert Sherbert's Sherbets with Aunt Bernice.

Aaron Slater was sitting in a corner booth with Sofia and Rosie. As usual, Aaron was doodling on a pad of paper. Aaron was always drawing. He said it helped him figure things out.

Aunt Bernice hugged Ada and headed back to the shop with her sherbet. Ada and Iggy slid into the booth with their friends.

"Did you find Pup?" asked Ada.

Sofia shook her head and sadly poked her ice cream with a spoon. "Aaron helped us look," she said.

"There weren't *any* dogs in the park," said Aaron. "It was weird."

"Aha!" cried Iggy. "That's proof! There *is* a pet thief!"

"A thief?" asked Aaron.

Iggy told them about the disappearing dogs.

Sofia gasped. "A thief stole Pup!" she said.

"We don't know that," said Ada. "It's not scientific to jump to conclusions. We need more facts."

"What I need is Pup!" said Sofia. "What if Pup is scared without me?"

"Thieves are so sneaky," said Aaron. He sketched a sneaky looking thief with a dog.

"A dog burglar!" said Sofia.

"He's a cat burglar, too," said Iggy.

Aaron flipped to a new page and sketched the burglar with a dog and a cat . . . and a mask . . . and an umbrella, in case it was raining . . . and a getaway car because Aaron liked drawing cars . . . and a helicopter and . . .

"A net!" said Sofia. "A thief would have a net and a coat with pockets for the little pets and . . ."

"What about a robot?" asked Rosie.

"A robot?!?" said Ada.

Aaron sketched a robot with a net.

"Can you make it sneakier?" asked Rosie. "The robot, I mean. Not the net."

Aaron flipped a page and drew a sneaky robot. His notebook was filling up fast.

"There are lots of missing pets," said Ada, "but we don't know there's a thief. Maybe we can use science to solve the mystery."

"Aliens use science!" said Iggy. "Maybe it's aliens!"

"In a spaceship!" said Aaron. "I love drawing spaceships."

Ada's friends were getting carried away.

"I don't know where the pets went," Ada said, "but we have to act carefully."

"We can carefully turn these sketches into posters," said Aaron. "And hang them around town!"

"That will help us catch the thief," said Iggy.

"Or robot aliens!" said Rosie.

Rosie, Sofia, and Iggy pulled out pencils and wrote warnings on Aaron's sketches.

Ada sighed quietly. Sofia noticed. She gently touched Ada's arm.

"We might be jumping to conclusions, Ada," said Sofia. "But we might be right, too. You don't know for sure that there's *not* a thief! We need to find Pup and Bricks fast. Posters could help."

"It can't *hurt* to start with posters," said Aaron. "Then we could do some science later."

"We can do both!" said Iggy. "I just want Bricks to come home now."

Ada smiled kindly at her friends. Sofia and Iggy were so upset, and the posters seemed to make them feel better. It probably wouldn't hurt. But would it help?

While her friends worked, Ada finished her ice cream. Then she slipped out of the booth and headed back to the Can You Dig It? shop.

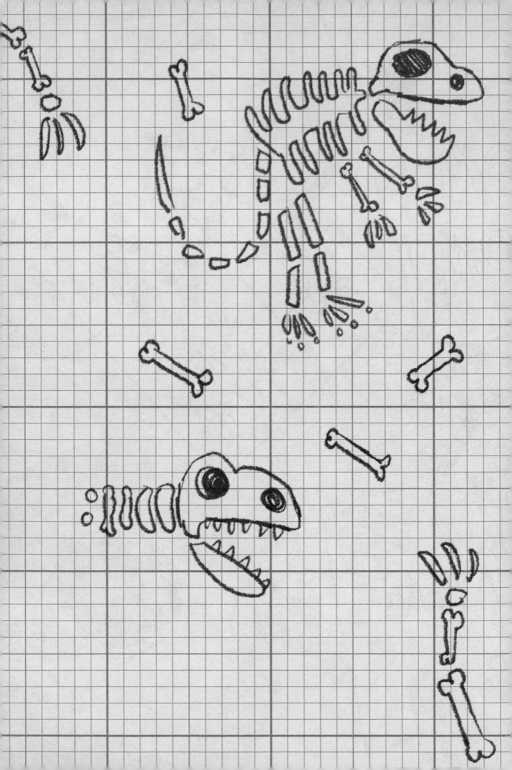

CHAPTER 5

A da plopped into Aunt Bernice's desk chair. Aunt Bernice looked up from the counter, where she was sorting tiny rocks. "What's wrong, sweetie?" she asked.

Ada told her about her friends and the silly-sounding thieves.

"Ahhh," said Aunt Bernice. "Are their imaginations running wild?"

Ada nodded.

Aunt Bernice looked closely at her niece. "And you wish they'd listen better?"

Ada paused, then nodded again.

Aunt Bernice opened the glass display case and carefully took out the dinosaur tooth. "It was a spoon, by the way," she said.

Ada looked at Aunt Bernice. "What was a spoon?" she asked.

"You asked about the shovel that dug this up," said Aunt Bernice. "I used a spoon."

"YOU dug up a dinosaur?" asked Ada. "By yourself?"

"I had help . . ." said Aunt Bernice. "Eventually."

She handed the tooth to Ada, who cradled it in her cupped hands. It was the most spectacular thing she had ever touched.

"Super zowie," she whispered.

Aunt Bernice continued. "One day, I saw that tip sticking out of the ground," she said. "Everyone said it was just another rock on the farm. But *I* knew what it was."

"What happened?" asked Ada.

"I got out my spoon and started digging!" said Aunt Bernice. "I dug out tiny bits of dirt and rock until the tooth was exposed. It took weeks. I was as careful and scientific as I could be. After that, I found two more teeth and three bones!"

"Did people listen then?" asked Ada.

"Oh yeah," Aunt Bernice said with a grin. "Dad phoned the paleontology department of the university. They didn't think a kid could find a dinosaur, but my dad told them what he'd learned from me."

"What was that?" asked Ada.

"Bones are bones. Facts are facts," said Aunt Bernice. "Science doesn't care if you believe in it or not. It just is.

"Dad was a smart man," she said. "He let the university dig for the fossils on one condition."

"What condition?" asked Ada.

"That I got to be the leader!" said Aunt Bernice.

"What?" asked Ada.

"Of course, Dr. Erica Harrow was *really* the leader," said Aunt Bernice, "but she made me her helper and taught me EVERYTHING! I haven't stopped digging since!"

"Where's the dinosaur now?" asked Ada.

"We sold it to a museum," said Aunt Bernice. "But I got to keep the tooth!"

"How old were you?" asked Ada.

Aunt Bernice pointed to a picture on a shelf.

"Old enough to know that bones are bones and facts are facts, and when you've got a dinosaur

tooth to dig, you get out your spoon and get diggin'. Even if you have to do it yourself!"

Ada suspected that Aunt Bernice wasn't talking about dinosaurs anymore.

"But my friends—" Ada started.

"Are lovely and smart and they care about you," said Aunt Bernice. "They will come around."

Ada handed the tooth back to Aunt Bernice. "But—"

"Well," said Aunt Bernice, "I suppose you could start cleaning display cases instead of figuring out what's happening to the pets in this town."

Aunt Bernice put back the tooth. When she turned around again, Ada was deep in thought, scribbling notes at the desk. Aunt Bernice could see the wheels of Ada's mind turning. Ada was so full of questions. So hungry for answers.

Aunt Bernice straightened the photo of the girl in the khaki hat, smiled, and went to the storeroom to sort more rocks, humming happily as she went.

CHAPTER 6

A da stared at her notebook. Questions filled her mind: Was there really a thief? Why were there so many missing pets? Why do people have pets? Which pet is the best? Can cats and dogs understand each other? Do mice really like cheese? Why does some cheese have holes in it? Does the air in cheese holes taste like cheese or air?

How do scientists figure things out? she wondered.

THE SCIENTIFIC METHOD

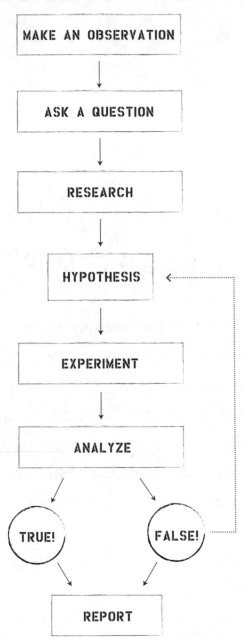

Ada already knew the answer to that question. Scientists have a scientific method to follow. Cleverly, they call it the scientific method.

Great name, thought Ada.

STEP 1: MAKE AN OBSERVATION.

That's my favorite part, thought Ada.

Observation: A lot of pets are missing in Blue River Creek.

STEP 2: ASK A QUESTION

That's my favorite part, too, she thought.

Question: Why are the pets missing?

STEP 3: RESEARCH

Research! thought Ada. *That's my most favorite part of all!*

Ada loved research. She spent every chance she got digging through Aunt Bernice's old encyclopedias. She loved their cracked leather covers with faded gold letters. They taught her about everything from aardvarks to zinnias.

Ada scanned the dusty brown volumes.

Where should I start? she wondered. *T for thief? Or P for pet? Or D for dog? Or . . .*

"Aha!" she said. "A for animal!"

Ada stood on her tiptoes and pulled down *Volume 1: Aar–Azy.*

She plopped the heavy book onto the desk with a thud and flipped through the pages. She jotted notes as she went. When she reached the end of the volume, Ada stacked it on the floor and pulled down the next one. Specks of dust floated down from the shelf and tickled her nose. She pushed away a sneeze and kept going.

Volume by volume, Ada worked her way through the alphabet. When she reached the end, her arms were sore, her notebook was full, and the stack of encyclopedias on the floor was twice as tall as she was.

And it was leaning.

Uh-oh! thought Ada.

She nudged volume 7 to the right and volume 14 to the left. She scooted volume 3 with her toe. The stack tilted this way. It tilted that way. It wibbled. It wobbled.

Ada wrapped her arms around the tower of books and a cloud of dust landed on her face.

"Ah—"

A sneeze began in her nose.

"Ahhhhhhhhh—"

It grew . . .

"Ahhhhhhhhhhhh—"

AND GREW!

"AAAAAHHHHHHHHHHHH—"

Suddenly, a red polka-dot handkerchief popped up in front of Ada's face. She grabbed it, whirled around, and—

"AHHH-CHOOOOOOOOOOOOOOOOOOOOOOOOO!"

At that moment, Ada realized that she was no longer holding the stack of books. She squeezed her eyes shut and braced herself for the crashing, clunking thud of encyclopedias.

She waited. And waited. Nothing happened. Ada carefully opened her eyes. She saw a set of perfectly stacked encyclopedias and four smiling friends.

"Best sneeze ever!" said Sofia.

"Great tower," said Iggy.

"It's a book sculpture!" said Aaron.

"Glad I had a spare hankie," said Rosie. "You can keep it."

Aunt Bernice stepped out of the storeroom. "Do you need some help, Ada?" she asked.

Ada looked at her friends and grinned.

"Nope!" she said. "I've got all the help I need!"

Aunt Bernice nodded.

"THAT," she said, "is a fact."

CHAPTER 7

We hung up the posters," said Sofia, "but I think you're right that we don't know for sure whether there's a thief. Science will help us figure out what happened."

"It just felt good to do something fast," said Iggy. "I really miss Bricks."

"I know," said Ada.

"How can we help?" asked Rosie.

Aaron looked nervously at the thick encyclopedias.

"Do we have to read all those?" Aaron asked. "It will take a long time with my dyslexia, but I'll try. Or maybe someone else can read them out loud and I'll do this."

Aaron sketched a picture of a giant ear.

Ada smiled. "Listening is the *perfect* place to start," she said.

Ada told her friends about the scientific method and the work she had done so far.

Observation: A lot of pets are missing in Blue River Creek.
Question: Why are the pets missing?
Research:

Ada held up her notebook. "Research helps us figure out an explanation for our observation," she said. "That's called a hypothesis."

"What did you learn?" asked Iggy.

"Lots of stuff," said Ada. "Look!"

- Dogs = First animal domesticated by people. Domesticated means breeding animals for the traits that are most helpful. Like tameness or lacking fear of humans or strength or speed.

- Dogs were bred for thousands and thousands of years to get different abilities, sizes, and traits. Dogs were bred for hunting, herding, sledding, swimming, and companionship.

- Dogs came from an ancient, extinct kind of wolf, which is not the same as the modern wolf.

- Dogs have the ability to understand and communicate with people more than any other animal.

"Wait," said Sofia. "Dogs are really great at understanding people?"

"Maybe a thief knew that and tricked the dogs

and Bricks into following them so they could steal the pets!" said Iggy.

"I think our hypothesis could be that there is a pet thief!" said Rosie.

Ada listened and thought and tapped on her chin and thought some more.

"Well . . ." she said. "I don't know if it's the strongest hypothesis, but it's a good one to start with."

"Start?" asked Aaron. "You mean we might need more than one?"

"That depends on how the next step goes," said Ada.

"What's the next step?" asked Aaron.

"My favorite part of all," said Ada. "We'll create an experiment to test our hypothesis!"

"How do we test it?" asked Rosie.

Ada smiled.

"That's what we're going to figure out!" she said. "Together!"

CHAPTER 8

The Questioneers brainstormed ideas for an hour. Finally, they drew up a plan. Aaron drew the pictures. Ada wrote the words. It looked like this:

1. The Pet Problem:
   a. Observation—Lots of pets are missing.
   b. Question—Why are the pets missing?
   c. Research—

RESEARCH IS IN HERE!

d. Hypothesis: A thief stole the pets.

e. Experiment: We will test our hypothesis by setting a trap for the thief. The trap will attract the thief with pet decoys, then take the thief's picture, then spray the thief with Stinkaroo (Mom's perfume + Dad's cologne + cabbage stew), so we can track the thief by the smell.

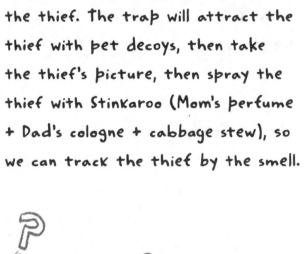

i. Rosie designs three decoys:

1. Goosie Talkie. Lets us listen to what's going on.

2. Toy cat that sprays Stinkaroo from tail.

3. Snappy the turtle, which takes Polaroid pictures when someone gets close.

ii. Iggy designs a house for the pet decoys.

iii. Aaron creates signs to point out where the pets are.

iv. Disguise ourselves during test so the thief doesn't see us.

v. Observe.

CHAPTER 9

Early the next morning, the Questioneers got busy. Before long, the perfect trap was set in Ada's front yard. It looked great and they were sure it would prove their hypothesis true or false.

The Questioneers put on their disguises and ducked out of sight. They waited. And waited. And waited.

Nothing happened. Rosie fussed with the dial on the Goosey-Talkie.

"I'm bored," she whispered.

"Me, too," whispered Sofia.

Just then, the Goosey-Talkie crackled. The Questioneers leaned in close.

CRACKLE . . . CRACKLE . . . QUACK . . .

"What did it say?" asked Aaron.

QUACK . . . QUACK . . .

Tap. Tap. Tap.

QUAAAAAAAAACK!

"Let's go look!" said Ada.

The disguised Questioneers tiptoed toward the pet house.

"Aha!" yelled Iggy, jumping out from behind his shrub.

"Gotcha!" yelled Sofia.

QUACK! QUACK!

A startled black duck quacked angrily at them and flew away.

"A duck?" said Ada.

"I don't think a duck would steal a dog," said Sofia.

"Or a cat," said Iggy.

"I could draw that!" said Aaron.

"Maybe we need a break," said Ada. "Let's go scientifically study my dad's cookies. We'll keep the Goosey-Talkie on in case the thief strikes."

The Questioneers parked their shrub disguises by the kitchen door, and soon they were eating chocolate chip caramel cookies at the table.

"I really love science," said Rosie. "Especially with cold milk."

Suddenly, the Goosey-Talkie handset crackled again.

"It's just the duck," said Ada.

Crackle . . . crackle . . .

"OUCH!"

"Ouch?" said Rosie.

"That duck speaks English!" said Sofia.

"THAT'S MY RACKET!"

"Uh-oh," said Ada. "That duck speaks Arthur!"

Arthur was Ada's brother. He loved playing tennis. What he did NOT love was Ada using his stuff in her science experiments. Especially his tennis racket.

"Uh-oh," said Ada. "I think he's going to—"

PSSSSSSSTTTTTTT

"Trip the trap?" asked Rosie.

Ada nodded.

"BLARGH! . . . P.U.!!!!! . . . ADA!!!!"

Moments later, a very angry, VERY stinky Arthur Twist stormed up the walk and into the house with his tennis racket in hand. A cloud of Stinkaroo wafted behind him.

"ADA!!!" he yelled, running through the

kitchen on his way to the shower. "I told you to stop using my tennis racket in your experiments!"

Arthur did not notice the glasses of milk on the kitchen table. Nor did he notice the new shrubs by the kitchen door.

CHAPTER 10

The shrubs sneaked outside and tiptoed toward the experiment. Ada peeked inside the pet house. The cat was out of Stinkaroo juice and the tennis racket was gone. Aaron had sprung the trap.

Ada jotted some notes and frowned. "This is what Rosie calls a Fabulous Flop," she said. "The worst part is that we didn't learn anything."

"We learned that science stinks!" said Aaron, waving his hand in front of his nose.

"But it tastes great!" said Sofia, munching on a cookie.

"I think the experiment *did* work a little," said Rosie. "It was an awesome trap. If it didn't catch a thief, then maybe there isn't one."

"Maybe," said Ada. "But we can't be certain. There *could* still be a thief, and our trap just didn't catch them before Arthur came in. And now we'll never know."

"What do you do when an experiment doesn't prove if your hypothesis is true or false?" asked Aaron.

Ada looked at the house. "The first thing we do," she said, "is get out of here before Arthur gets done with that shower!"

Faster than a cloud of Stinkaroo in a windstorm, the Questioneers were gone.

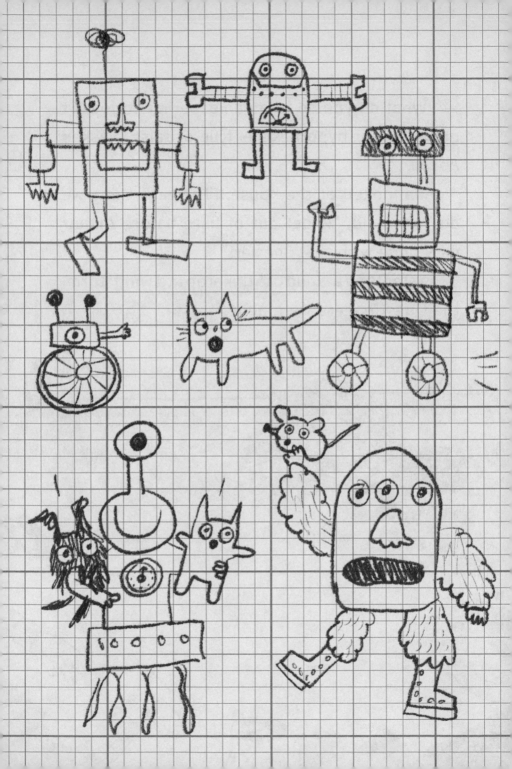

CHAPTER II

When they reached the Can You Dig It? shop, Aunt Bernice was on the phone.

"Oh . . . That *is* scary," she said into the handset. "Don't worry . . . It's okay . . . Bye!"

She hung up the phone.

"What's going on?" asked Ada.

"That was Ms. Good," said Aunt Bernice. "She canceled our coffee because she's scared out of her wits. She's afraid that robot aliens are after her pets! Now why would she think that?" She looked at the Questioneers.

"Because of our posters?" asked Aaron.

Aunt Bernice nodded.

"But we didn't mean to scare anybody," said Sofia. "We just wanted to warn people!"

"Seems that you did both," said Aunt Bernice.

"We didn't think it would hurt to warn people," said Iggy.

"I know you meant well," said Aunt Bernice, "but spreading stories without facts can always harm someone. Get facts first."

"We should take the posters down until we know who the thief is," said Rosie.

"We still haven't proven there *is* a thief," said Ada.

"There has to be," said Iggy. "Bricks wouldn't just run away."

"Neither would Pup!" said Sofia.

"But there might be another reason," said Ada.

"What happened with your experiment?" asked Aunt Bernice.

"Arthur happened!" said Ada.

"Ada?" said Aunt Bernice. "Did you use his stuff again?"

"Well . . ." said Ada. "It was for science, but it didn't even help. The experiment didn't prove the hypothesis true *or* false. Now we're out of Stinkaroo and tennis rackets, so we can't even try again."

"Can the scientific method help us?" asked Rosie.

"Good idea!" Ada said. She thumbed through her notebook. "Here's our observation. 'A lot of pets are missing in Blue River Creek.'"

"That's still true," said Rosie.

Ada nodded. "Question," she said. "Why are the pets missing?"

"That's still the big question," said Aaron. "The next step is research."

"Ada," asked Iggy, "what else did you learn in your research?"

Ada laid her notebook on the table and the kids gathered around. They flipped through the pages.

Art Deco architecture became famous in 1925 at the international show in Paris.

Bibble-babble was a very common word 600 years ago. It meant senseless talk.

The Chrysler Building was built in New York City in 1928.

Dogs can sniff and breathe at the same time.

Dogs have eighteen muscles controlling their ears.

Dolphins sleep with one eye open.

A cloud can weigh more than a million pounds.

 Fungus is not fun.

More than 800 languages are spoken in Papua New Guinea.

A group of zebras is called a "dazzle."

"Art Deco architecture!" said Iggy. "That's my favorite! And so is Art Nouveau architecture! And Gothic architecture! And . . ."

"The moon is 238,900 miles from Earth!" read Rosie.

"Giraffes have the longest tongue of any land animal!" read Aaron.

"Ada, how does that help us find Pup and Bricks?" asked Sofia. "Shouldn't the research be about missing pets?"

"Oh . . ." said Ada. She wrinkled her brow and tapped her chin. "You're right, Sofia! There was so much interesting stuff in the encyclopedias that I forgot what I was researching." Ada frowned. "I guess I got carried away," she said quietly.

Aaron flipped open his notebook to a picture of an alien robot thief scooping a bunch of kittens into a big purple net. "It's okay, Ada," he said. "We all did!"

CHAPTER 12

"A aron is right," said Sofia. "We *all* got carried away. Maybe we can try again."

Ada smiled. "Okay," she said. "Let's start fresh research. Where can we find data about the missing pets?"

"The pet shop!" said Rosie.

"Let's do it!" said Ada.

Three minutes later, the Questioneers were standing before the wall of posters in the back of the pet shop. There were a dozen new posters

since yesterday. Ada jotted in her notebook as she and the Questioneers studied each poster.

"Is there a pattern?" asked Ada.

"Animals with four legs?" asked Aaron.

"No," said Ada. "Here's a bird!"

"A bird!?!" cried Rosie. "I know my bird is safe because Gizmo is visiting Great-Aunt Rose, but the fact that birds are going missing is too close for comfort."

Ada thought about her own cat, Bunsen Burner, who was at home.

Was she safe? Was any pet in Blue River Creek safe?

Was there any pattern to the missing animals? There were mammals, reptiles, and birds. There were animals with feathers. Animals with fur. Animals with scales. There was even a turtle. But there was not a pattern.

Ada tapped her chin and stared at the board. "There has to be some kind of pattern," she said. "But what?"

"Aha!" said Aaron. "That's the wrong question! The right question is *Where?*"

CHAPTER 13

Aaron pointed at a delivery map near the fish tanks.

"Sofia," he said, "where was Pup when you saw him last?"

"In my yard," said Sofia. "I was about to give him a bath, so I took off his collar and went to put it on the porch. When I came back, he was gone."

She pointed to the map. Aaron marked the spot with an X.

"What about Bricks?" asked Aaron.

Iggy pointed to his street and Aaron made another X on the map.

"Here's one from Maple Street," said Ada.

"And two from Oak Avenue," said Rosie.

Aaron marked the spots.

They went from poster to poster, marking the map with each location they found.

"Look!" said Aaron. "That's it!"

Ada looked at the map, but she only saw a bunch of red Xs scattered over the map. She tilted her head left and right and squinted. The map made no sense.

"I don't see anything," she said.

"Exactly!" said Aaron, waving his hand over half of the map.

"There's nothing there!" said Rosie.

"Ohhhh," said Iggy. He squinted at the map. "I still don't get it," he said.

"Look!" said Aaron. "There are no missing

pets over here. All the Xs start at the pet shop and go that way."

"It's a route!" said Sofia.

Aaron traced his finger along the map.

"Oh," said Ada. "That is *very* interesting."

"So is this!" Rosie said. "It's the Reading Buddies!" She showed them a poster of four animals in vests in front of the library.

"Moby Duck!" said Iggy, pointing at the black duck in the photo.

"He was the duck at your house, Ada!" said Aaron. "We didn't recognize him without his vest!"

"Did Moby Duck get stolen and escape?" asked Iggy. "Or was the thief nearby when we were at Ada's house?"

A look of shock ran over Ada's face. "Oh no," she said. "If there *is* a thief and that thief stole Moby Duck, they were by my house! Bunsen Burner is inside! We need to save her!"

Bunsen Burner

CHAPTER 14

The Questioneers ran out of the pet shop toward Ada's house as fast as they could. They arrived by the mailbox, out of breath.

"Phew," said Rosie. "Look! Bunsen Burner is safe!"

Bunsen Burner was curled up in the front window, blinking lazily and licking her paw.

Iggy poked his head into the pet house and pulled it right back out again. "P.U.!" he said. "It's still stinky in there. Stinkaroo is powerful stuff!"

"That was the point," said Ada. "The spray was supposed to stink up the thief. Not Arthur."

"Well . . ." said Rosie. "We didn't see a thief. But I know who might have!"

"Snappy!" said Sofia. "We forgot to check Snappy!" She reached into the pet house and pulled out Snappy, the robot turtle, and carefully lifted the turtle's tail.

WHIRRRRR.

BRRRRRRR.

BUZZZZZ.

DING!

A narrow strip of paper slid out from the turtle's bottom shell. Then another.

CRUNCH

CHAPTER 15

Look!" said Iggy. "It *is* Moby Duck!

"That's Hamlet's tail!" said Aaron.

"That's Nicky," said Ada. "He belongs to Ms. Good."

"Maybe she stole the pets!" said Sofia.

"No!" said Ada. "She's really nice and she already has a dog. Why would she steal pets?"

"Well," said Sofia, "she buys *a lot* of pet food."

Ada frowned. The thought of Ms. Good stealing pets was very upsetting. She knew that could not be the answer.

"Look at that," said Aaron. "It's a purple sleeve."

"The pet store clerk was wearing purple," said Sofia. "Maybe she did it!"

"We can't just—" Ada began.

CRUNCH.

She stepped back.

CRUNCH.

"Ugh!" she said, lifting her foot. "What is that?"

Crunchy brown crumbs stuck to the bottom of her shoe.

"It's one of these!" said Iggy, picking up a

small, triangular brown object from the edge of the sidewalk.

"What is it?" asked Aaron.

"That," said Ada, "is a clue!"

The Questioneers spread out looking for more crunchy triangles.

"Here's one!" said Sofia.

"And here!" called Aaron, who had walked farther down the sidewalk. "There's another one!"

"It's a trail of pet treats," said Aaron. "And it's heading that way!"

CHAPTER 16

The Questioneers followed the trail past Ada's house. Every few feet, they found another treat.

"This reminds me of Hansel and Gretel," said Iggy. "Will it end at a witch's cottage made of dog food instead of candy?"

"That would be scary," said Rosie. "And it would taste awful."

"Unless you were a dog," said Sofia with a worried look. "Pup would love that."

Ada was sure they were not going to find a witch's house made of dog food. But she wondered what they might find at the end of the trail. Was someone trying to lure pets away from home? Who? Why? The idea was a little scary.

"Maybe we should stick together," she said.

The Questioneers nodded and continued their search.

They reached the end of the block, then another. The sidewalk ended at Green Goose Road. To the left, Green Goose Road ran to the Mysterious Mansion. To the right, it headed out of Blue River Creek. Ahead, there was an overgrown private lane.

"Which way do we go?" asked Sofia.

"Follow the treats!" said Iggy.

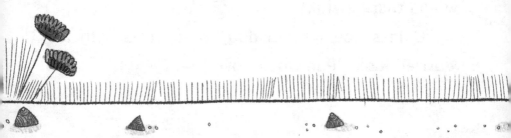

The Questioneers spread out.

"Over here!" called Rosie from the lane. "I see a bunch!"

The Questioneers followed the treats. The lane dwindled to two worn tracks, then dissolved into a narrow footpath surrounded by high weeds. A few broken stems showed that someone had walked this path recently.

They walked single file down the path. A crow perched on a scraggly shrub and glared at them with its dark, beady eyes.

CAW! CAW!

Aaron shuddered. The crow flew off.

"I don't like it here," he said. "Should we go get some—"

WOOF!

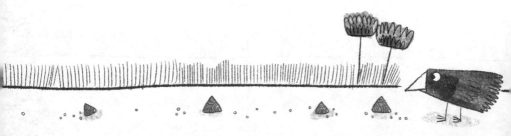

"Listen!" said Ada.

WOOF!

"That's Pup!" said Sofia, running toward the bark.

"Sofia!" yelled Rosie. "Come back!"

Rosie ran after Sofia. The others followed.

The path curved to the right. Then to the left. The trees grew thicker, blocking out the sun. The shadowy trail curved again. Suddenly, it ended at a weather-worn wooden arch above a rusted iron gate. Ada looked at the peeling letters on the arch and gasped.

"Is it a warning?" asked Aaron.

"No," said Ada, sadly. "It's something worse."

CHAPTER 17

"It's a name," Ada said.

"Doesn't it say, 'Be good'?" asked Aaron. "That's kind of a warning."

"Not exactly," said Ada. "It says *B.E. Good.* I think that means Beverly Elaine Good."

"See!" said Sofia. "I knew it!"

"But it doesn't make sense," said Ada. "I can't believe she—"

CREEEEEAAAAK . . .

"Look!" said Rosie.

The Questioneers peered through the iron gate at a faint path, which led to a weathered red barn. The barn door was closing with a loud creaking noise. It stopped slightly ajar. Soft light spilled out of the narrow opening.

A loud bark erupted inside the barn.

BOW WOW WOW.

"Pup!" said Sofia.

Another dog joined in. And another. A loud meow rose up in the midst of the barks. It was joined by a chorus of cat yowls.

"Bricks!" said Iggy.

The Questioneers ran through the gap in the iron gate and sneaked to the barn. Their hearts raced. They pressed against the crack of light and peeked inside. They could make out golden bales of hay lit dimly by a suspended light bulb.

QUACK!

OINK!

WOOOOOOOF!

MEOWWWWW!

A cacophony of animal sounds split the air. Then, suddenly, the Questioneers heard another sound. It was close by.

Grrrrrrrrrrr.

"Sorry," said Iggy. "My stomach is growling. I think I'm hungry."

Grrrrrrrrrrrrrrrrr!

Iggy poked his stomach. "Wait . . . that's not my stom—"

GRRRRRRRRRRRRRRRR.

The Questioneers wheeled around. Behind them stood a growling, blue-eyed Siberian husky.

GRRRRRRRRRR-WOOOOOOOOOOOOOOOOF!

The Questioneers pressed their backs against the barn door, trying to put some space between them and the howling dog. Its piercing blue eyes were locked on them. Its sharp, white teeth glowed in the dim light.

"Nice Nicky," said Ada. "Remember me?"

GRRRRRRRRRR-WOOOOOOOOOOOOOOOOF!

"Nice doggy," said Iggy, squeezing his eyes shut. "Nice dog—"

CREEEEEEAAAAAAAAK!

Suddenly, the barn door slid away behind them and the Questioneers tumbled backward into the earthy-smelling dim cavern of the barn.

Observation:

Ms. Good has the missing pets!

Question:

Why ????

CHAPTER 18

The blue-eyed dog leaped over them and bounded onto a row of hay bales, where a dozen other dogs and almost as many cats sat together howling and meowing as loudly as they could. Next to them sat a curly-tailed pig. Above them, a black duck quacked from a rafter.

A woman in purple stood above the Questioneers. She waved a tiny, pointed black stick at them like a wand.

"Get back, burglars!" she yelled. "Robots!

Aliens! Shoo!" She waved the tiny baton at the heap of Questioneers, then backed up toward the hay bales and stood boldly in front of the yowling animals, as if to protect them. "Shoo, burglars! Get out!"

"We're not burglars!" said Sofia.

"Just what a burglar would say!" said Ms. Good. "Shoo!"

The Questioneers scrambled to their feet.

"Ms. Good!" said Ada. "I'm Ada Twist. Remember me?"

"Ada?" asked Ms. Good. "Bernice's Ada?"

"Yes, ma'am," said Ada. "And these are my friends."

"Oh goodness! Quick!" said Ms. Good. "Close the barn door! There are thieves around! Alien robots! It's not safe! What are you kids doing out here?"

"There aren't any aliens or robots," said Aaron.

"There are!" said Ms. Good. "I saw their scary pictures around town! And they are NOT going to steal my pets!"

CHAPTER 19

Your pets?" asked Sofia.

"Yes!" said Ms. Good. "People abandoned them at the edge of town. Nicky and I rescued them, and we won't let thieves get them!"

"But—" Iggy said.

"It's not safe out there with thieves about!" said Ms. Good. "I'll get you kids home. But first, I have to finish something."

With that, Ms. Good turned around and flicked her conductor's baton in the air. Silence!

Every animal sat at attention. She flicked the baton again.

Miss Good lifted her chin and opened her mouth.

The most beautiful note swirled through the air.

LAAAAAAAAAAAAAAAAAAAA AAAAAA . . .

Suddenly, the animals joined in.

WOOOOOOOOF-MEEOOOOOW- QUAAAACKKK-OINKKKKK!

The strange animal song filled the air. It was moody. It was mysterious. And it was musical!

Ms. Good sang and swished the baton this way and that. The animals yowled louder. Then softer. Higher. Then lower. Finally, Ms. Good lowered the baton.

And for a moment, there was silence. It was a silence that—for just a heartbeat—held the beauty of all the music that had come before.

It was the most beautiful silence Ada had ever heard.

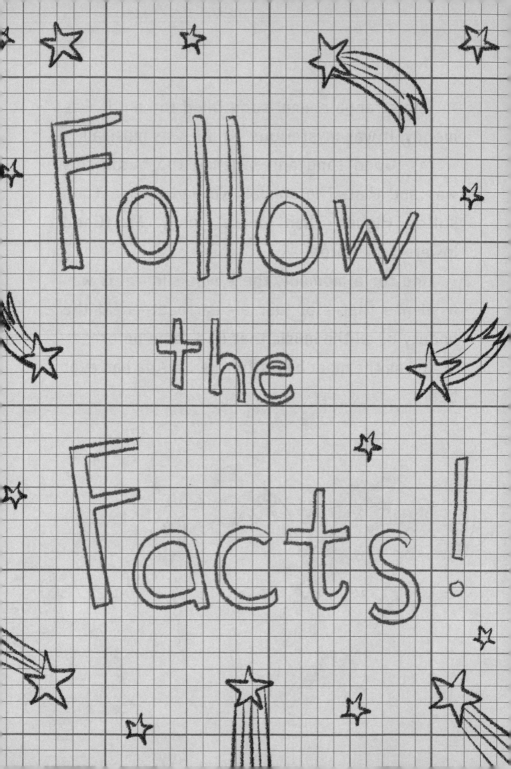

Follow the Facts!

CHAPTER 20

The Questioneers were speechless. Ms. Good took a bow and waved her arm in recognition of the chorus.

"Bravo!" she said.

Nicky grumbled.

"Yes!" said Ms. Good. "You ARE a good boy!"

Ms. Good reached into her purse and pulled out a triangular pet treat. Nicky gobbled it down and licked his chops. Ms. Good went to each animal. She praised their singing, scratched their chins, and gave them each a treat.

She reached Bricks. "Such an improvement, Meowzart!" she said.

"That's not Meowzart!" cried Iggy. "That's *MY* cat, Bricks!"

Bricks chomped down on the treat, stretched lazily, then walked over to Iggy, who scooped him up and hugged him tight.

"And that's *MY* dog, Pup!" said Sofia. She held out her arms and Pup jumped into them and licked her face. Sofia blinked back a tear as she clutched her dog. "I missed you so much," she said.

Ms. Good froze. A confused look passed over her face. "Pup? Bricks?" she said. "I don't understand. These animals were all abandoned on my lane."

Sofia's cheeks got hot. That always happened when she got upset. She clutched Pup tight. "Pup vanished yesterday from my yard," she said. "I would never leave him!"

"And Bricks has been my cat forever!" said Iggy. "I would never abandon him!"

"And that's Moby Duck!" said Rosie. "He's one of the Library Reading Buddies!"

The duck flew down from the rafter and pecked Ms. Good's shoelace. She handed him a treat and gently stroked his feathers. "No, no!" said Ms. Good. "This is Duck Ellington! Someone dumped him here today. Right outside my gate! But he's welcome here. He and Piginini are already part of the family."

"Piginini?" said Aaron. "That's Hamlet!"

"No, my dear. *Hamlet* is a play," said Ms. Good. "These are musical animals. And their names reflect that."

Aaron handed Ms. Good the poster of the missing Reading Buddies. "We found this in the Pet Palace."

She looked at it and looked at the animals. She looked back at the poster and gasped. A look of horror passed over her face.

"Oh my," she said. "I don't understand. Did I . . . Could I have . . . But . . ."

She sat down on the bale of hay. Nicky rested his head on her lap. The old woman absently scratched his chin. "Oh my," she said. "I'm a thief and I didn't even know it! If only I had gone inside the Pet Palace instead of making them load my wagon, I would have seen this and figured it out. I just hated those fish tanks."

A tear rolled down her cheek. She sniffled. She opened her purse and pulled out a handkerchief to wipe away a tear. Nicky nuzzled her arm, and she took another treat from her purse. He gobbled down the treat and laid his head back in her lap.

Once again, the barn fell silent.

"I never meant to . . ." she started. "I thought I was helping. People have always abandoned animals out here."

The Questioneers did not know what to say or how to comfort the old woman. Rosie looked at Iggy who looked at Aaron who looked at Sofia who looked at—

"Hey!" Sofia said. "Where's Ada?"

CHAPTER 21

Ada was behind the bales of hay, looking at a large stack of dog treat bags and an empty wagon.

She tapped her chin and thought. Suddenly, she smiled. She joined the others and sat down by Ms. Good.

"I think I know what happened," said Ada. "I've researched the situation and I have a new hypothesis. But we need to test it. Can you help us?"

"Oh," said Ms. Good. "I think I've done enough. What if I accidentally steal more pets? I'm so ashamed!"

"If my hypothesis is right," said Ada, "we'll prove that you didn't steal ANY pets!"

She stood up and held out her hand to Ms. Good.

Ms. Good paused for a moment, then she wiped away her tear and grabbed Ada's hand. "You remind me of your great-aunt," she said, standing up. "Bernice is always out to find answers. I'll help if I can."

CHAPTER 22

L et's get started!" said Ada.

"What's the hypothesis?" asked Rosie.

"For now," said Ada, "it's a secret."

"Okay, Ada!" said Aaron. "We're listening to you! Just tell us how to help!"

Rosie, Iggy, and Aaron loaded bags of pet food into the wagon and opened the barn door.

"What now?" asked Sofia.

"Observe what happens," said Ada.

Together, Ada Twist and Ms. Good grabbed

the wagon handle and headed down the shadowy path. Nicky trotted happily behind the wagon.

It was almost dusk and the trail was dim. They silently made their way to the gate and onto the lane.

Ms. Good looked around at the overgrown lane and peeling paint and sighed. "This place has gotten away from me," she said. "I was going

to fix it up when I retired, but I can't seem to find the energy. I don't know where the days go."

"The bees probably like it," said Ada, trying to cheer her up.

"You're kind like Bernice, too," said Ms. Good.

They crossed Green Goose Road and headed toward Ada's house.

Ada did not dare look at Nicky as they walked. She did not want to influence the experiment. She began to worry whether the experiment would work, but soon, she heard a soft crunching sound and a faint *tick-tick-tick*ing that continued as they headed toward downtown Blue River Creek. Ms. Good was too lost in thought to notice.

Finally, they reached the pet shop.

"We're here," said Ms. Good. "What do we do now?"

"The only thing we can do," said Ada. "We wait."

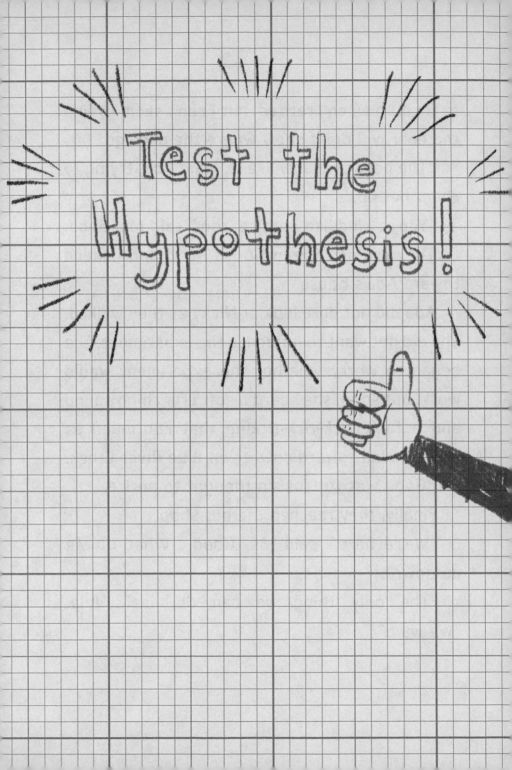

CHAPTER 23

They waited. And waited and waited. Nothing happened.

Ms. Good sighed. "Ada," she said. "I should go inside and tell them that I stole the pets." She sniffled. "I'm so embarrassed. Nothing has gone at all the way I imagined after I retired. But this is just too much." She turned toward the pet shop door.

"Wait!" said Ada. "Do you hear that?"

"What is it?" asked Ms. Good.

"The sound of science!" said Ada. "The experiment is working!"

Ms. Good looked around. "I don't see anything," she said.

"Listen!" said Ada. "It's—"

QUAAAAAACK!

Ada looked up just as a big black duck came in for a landing right on top of the wagon.

QUAAAACK!

"Duck Ellin—" Ms. Good started. "I mean Moby Duck."

A moment later, a pig with a curly tail waddled up the sidewalk toward them. He led a parade of animals, followed by the Questioneers. Every few steps, the animals stopped and nibbled something off the ground.

"Ada," said Ms. Good. "What's going on?"

"Science!" said Ada. "Science is going on! My hypothesis is true!"

"What *was* your hypothesis?" asked Iggy.

"My hypothesis was that there was NO thief," said Ada. "Nobody stole the animals. They all just followed treats and ended up at Ms. Good's barn."

"What treats?" asked Ms. Good.

"The treats that Nicky left behind the wagon," said Ada. "Look!"

She pointed to a nearly empty bag of dog treats on the wagon. The plastic was riddled with holes just like the holes in Ms. Good's purse. The corner of the pet food bag was gone. A trail of triangular treats littered the sidewalk as far as they could see.

"But how—" Ms. Good started.

She looked at Nicky, who grumbled at her.

"Oh, Nicky!" she said.

"Your purse was the clue," said Ada. "Or data, as we call it in science. Nicky chewed off the corner of the bags and left a trail of treats wherever you went. The animals followed it to your barn."

"Oh my!" said Ms. Good. "Then I thought they were abandoned and hid them in the barn for safety." She gasped. "But I wasn't keeping them safe at all," she said. "I was petnapping them!"

Just then, the pet shop clerk came out of the store. "What's going on?" she asked. "Can I get you more bags of pet food, Ms. Good?"

"Oh no," said Ms. Good, sadly.

Ada explained what had happened.

"Can you help these pets find their families?" asked Ms. Good. "I know they must be very worried about them." She paused and smiled sadly. "Tell them that they have very good pets ... and wonderful singers. And that I am so, so sorry."

The clerk went into the store and came back with a stack of posters from the wall. Rosie and Aaron dug through the posters, matching phone numbers with missing pets and making a plan with the clerk.

Sofia and Iggy happily hugged their pets.

"You were right all along, Ada!" said Sofia. "I'm glad there wasn't a thief!"

"Science wins!" said Aaron. "Even if it is stinky!"

"Good job," said Rosie. "That scientific method really worked!"

OINK!

Hamlet sniffed Rosie's shoe.

OINK!

"I think he's hungry," said Rosie. "I'll take the Reading Buddies back to the library."

"I've got Bricks," said Iggy.

"I've got Pup," said Sofia.

"The rest can stay here at the shop until we find their families," said the clerk.

"I'll draw posters to help find their families," said Aaron. "No alien robots. I promise."

As the others made plans, one Questioneer was quiet. Ada stood to the side and watched as the old woman with a wagon and the fluffy-tailed dog silently walked down the sidewalk.

They turned the corner and were gone.

When Ada got home, she curled up in the Thinking Chair. Bunsen Burner climbed onto her lap. As always, questions filled Ada's mind. Usually, she shared them with her cat, who listened but rarely answered. Tonight, though, Ada sat quietly, listening to the soothing rumble of the purring cat.

Ada thought about the missing pets. About her friends and Aunt Bernice. She thought about the scientific method. And about the beautiful music in the barn.

But mostly, Ada thought about Ms. Good and Nicky walking sadly home together in the deepening shadows. In silence.

CHAPTER 24

The next morning, Ada was in a quiet mood.

"Very old penny for your thoughts," said Aunt Bernice, handing Ada a very old penny that she'd dug out of the yard.

"I'm thinking about Ms. Good," said Ada.

"Yesterday was hard for her," said Aunt Bernice.

"I think she was sad long before the pets showed up," said Ada.

"Maybe," said Aunt Bernice.

"But you thought she would have fun when she retired," said Ada.

"I did," said Aunt Bernice. "But you can't always know what's going on in someone's world. Sometimes, big life changes can throw us for a loop.

"Ms. Good loved her work and she was very good at it," Aunt Bernice added. "I think she feels lost without it. She used to spend every day with hundreds of people. Now, it's just her and the animals. Maybe she feels lonely or sad."

Ada sat quietly for a moment. "I didn't expect to find someone like her when we were looking for a pet thief," she said.

"It's the funny thing about digging," said Aunt Bernice. "You never know what you'll find."

Ada looked up at her great aunt. She wasn't talking about digging at all.

"Can we do something to help Ms. Good?" Ada asked. "Maybe then she won't be so lonely or sad."

"I'll check on her this afternoon," said Aunt Bernice. "Do you want to come with me?"

Ada nodded.

Aunt Bernice went back to the counter.

Ada sat at the desk and thought. Were there ways she and her friends could help Ms. Good? She grabbed a piece of paper and started a list.

Help in her garden
Bake her a treat
Sing her a song
Take Nicky for a walk
Start a "Singing Buddies" program at the library
. . . . .

Ada's list grew longer and longer, but was it helpful? Or was it like yesterday's encyclopedia research? Fun and interesting, but not very useful.

So much had happened in the last two days. But what had she learned?

Ada made a new list:

What I learned:
Stinkaroo is VERY stinky.
Stinky Arthur = Cranky Arthur
Naked ducks look alike.
Pigs are good singers.
Do the research right.
Gather facts first!

Ada wanted to help, but she didn't know how. Ms. Good was not a science experiment. But science was how Ada made sense of things. Just like Aaron made sense of things by drawing pictures.

Ada paused.

Suddenly, she knew exactly what to do.

"Super-duper zowie!" she said. "That's it!"

Ada shuffled the papers on the desk. Where had she put it?

"Aha!" she said, uncovering one of Aaron's pictures.

Ada Twist looked at the picture and knew exactly how she and Aunt Bernice could help Ms. Good. They could listen.

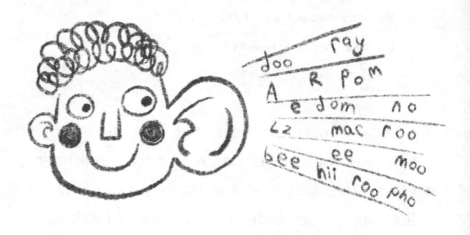

And that's exactly what they did.

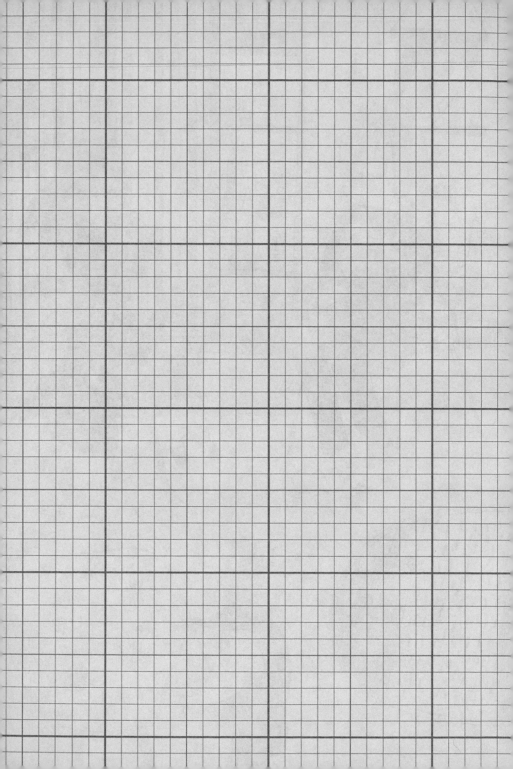

FOLLOW THE FACTS!

Great-Aunt Bernice taught Ada something very important about facts. Facts are real whether people understand them or believe in them. Facts are real even if people choose to ignore them. That's a good thing! It means that we can understand what's going on if we follow the facts.

Many professions follow the facts. Accountants use data to understand how much money a company has. Journalists follow facts and evidence to understand and report the news. If a story is true, other journalists can also follow the facts. If a news story is fake, there will not be facts to support it. (Helpful hint: Gathering news from a wide range of sources will help you identify the real story!)

Scientists like Ada sort fiction from fact through research and testing—through experiments!

AS A MATTER OF FACT

Is that a fact?
What does a fact do?
It helps us determine
what's false and what's true.

A fact isn't made up
or what we might feel.
A fact can be proven
and that makes it real.

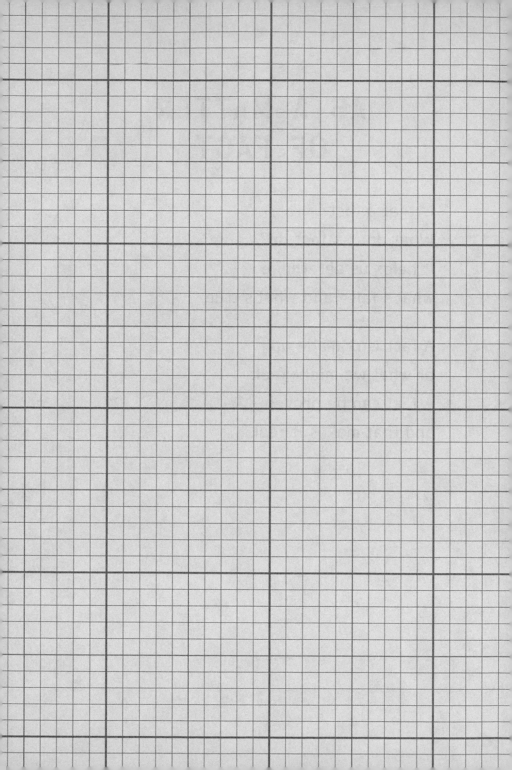

HOW TO LISTEN!

Everyone thinks they are great at conversations, but really, few people are. The key is being a good listener. When we truly listen to others, we make new friends as we find common interests.

Being good at conversations takes practice and effort. The focus of every conversation should be understanding the other person!

Here are some ideas to help you:

1. Pay attention. Look at the person who is talking with you. It shows respect and helps you understand what they are saying better.
2. Listen. Really and truly listen to the other person. Listening means thinking about what the other person says.
3. Ask questions. "What?" "Why?" "How?"
4. Listen to the answers. Take an interest in them.

5. In your own words, try to sum up what the other person said. This shows that you understand them. If you don't understand, ask them to explain what they mean.
6. Ask a question about something you learned.
7. Ask more questions and listen to the answers.
8. Now and then, connect their answers with things you know. Share your connections.
9. Ask more questions!
10. Always be willing to say, "I don't know" or "Could you explain that?" This shows you care about the conversation, and you might learn something new, too!
11. Remember, smart people ask questions!

THE ALLOSAURUS

The *Allosaurus* was a beast
that lived so long ago
with sawlike teeth inside its head
and claws upon its toes.
There was nothing it loved more
than chomping on an herbivore.

Alas, like every dinosaur,
the allosaur
is no
more.

People who study dinosaurs are called *paleontologists.* They learn a lot about dinosaurs from the teeth they unearth. Dinosaur skeletons and teeth offer clues about how the animals looked and even how they hunted and behaved. Herbivores were plant eaters. Carnivores were meat eaters.

Many long-necked plant-eating dinosaurs used their slender teeth to strip leaves from trees and swallowed the leaves whole. They did not have cheeks for storing food or grinding teeth to break up the food. They might have swallowed stones to grind the plants in their stomachs. Some short-necked herbivores, like the *Iguanodon,* used its flat back teeth to grind plants before swallowing.

The *Allosaurus* was a massive meat-eating dinosaur that weighed over 3,300 pounds. It lived in the Late Jurassic period. That was about 150 million years ago! *Allosaurus* teeth were covered with hard enamel. Each tooth had sharp, sawlike edges that cut through the meat of its prey. Sometimes it would lose teeth while hunting, but they constantly grew back. *Allosaurus* teeth

were between 2 and 4 inches long, while *T. rex* teeth could be up to 12 inches long!

Researchers believe that the *T. rex* would grab prey with its strong jaws and pull them down. The *Allosaurus* was much smaller and had a different way of hunting. Its jaws were very large but were not extremely strong. In fact, they were weaker than those of modern alligators, lions, or leopards.

Because of this, the allosaur was less likely to grab its prey and pull it down. Instead, it took bites out of the herbivores it hunted. It chomped down then moved its head up and down so its teeth could saw into its prey. Then, it pulled out chunks of meat. Sometimes it would kill the prey and sometimes it would just weaken it.

They really got their lunch to go!

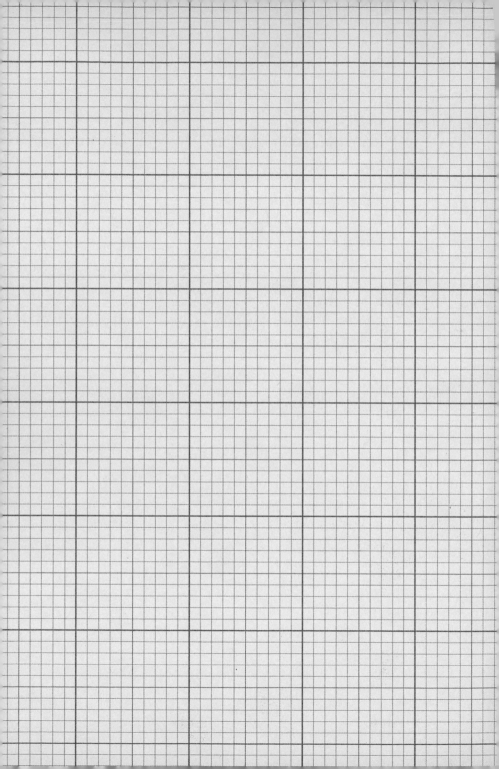